DEAR MOUSE FRIENDS, WELCOME TO THE

STONE AGE!

WELCOME TO THE STONE AGE . . . AND THE WORLD OF THE CAVEMICE!

CAPITAL: OLD MOUSE CITY

POPULATION: WE'RE NOT SURE. (MATH DOESN'T EXIST YET!) BUT BESIDES CAVEMICE, THERE ARE PLENTY OF DINOSAURS, <u>WAY</u> TOO MANY SABER-TOOTHED TIGERS, AND FEROCIOUS CAVE BEARS — BUT NO MOUSE HAS EVER HAD THE COURAGE TO COUNT THEM!

TYPICAL FOOD: PETRIFIED CHEESE SOUP

NATIONAL HOLIDAY: GREAT ZAP DAY, WHICH CELEBRATES THE DISCOVERY OF FIRE. RODENTS EXCHANGE GRILLED CHEESE SANDWICHES ON THIS HOLIDAY.

NATIONAL DRINK: MAMMOTH MILKSHAKES

CLIMATE: Unpredictable, WITH FREQUENT METEOR SHOWERS

cheese soup

milkshake

MONEY

SEASHELLS OF ALL SHAPES AND SIZES

MEASUREMENT

THE BASIC UNIT OF MEASUREMENT IS BASED ON THE LENGTH OF THE TAIL OF THE LEADER OF THE VILLAGE. A UNIT CAN BE DIVIDED INTO A HALF TAIL OR QUARTER TAIL. THE LEADER IS ALWAYS READY TO PRESENT HIS TAIL WHEN THERE IS A DISPUTE.

THE CAVEMICE

Geronimo

Trap

Thea

Benjamin

Bugsy Wugsy

Hercule Poirat

Grandma Ratrock

Geronimo Stilton

CAVEMICE

THE FAST AND
THE FROZEN

Scholastic Inc.

ISBN 978-0-545-64291-0

Based on an original idea by Elisabetta Dami.

www.geronimostilton.com

Published by Scholastic Inc., 557 Broadway, New York, NY 10012. SCHOLASTIC and associated logos are trademarks and/or registered trademarks of Scholastic Inc.

Stilton is the name of a famous English cheese. It is a registered trademark of the Stilton Cheese Makers' Association. For more information, go to www.stiltoncheese.com.

Text by Geronimo Stilton
Original title *Per mille mammut, mi si gela la coda!*
Cover by Flavio Ferron
Illustrations by Giuseppe Facciotto (design) and Daniele Verzini (color)
Graphics by Marta Lorini

Special thanks to Tracey West
Translated by Julia Heim
Interior design by Becky James

12 11 10   18 19/0

Printed in the U.S.A.   40
First printing, February 2014

MANY AGES AGO, ON PREHISTORIC MOUSE ISLAND, THERE WAS A VILLAGE CALLED OLD MOUSE CITY. IT WAS INHABITED BY BRAVE *RODENT SAPIENS* KNOWN AS THE CAVEMICE.

DANGERS SURROUNDED THE MICE AT EVERY TURN: EARTHQUAKES, METEOR SHOWERS, FEROCIOUS DINOSAURS, AND FIERCE GANGS OF SABER-TOOTHED TIGERS. BUT THE BRAVE CAVEMICE FACED IT ALL WITH A SENSE OF HUMOR, AND WERE ALWAYS READY TO LEND A HAND TO OTHERS.

HOW DO I KNOW THIS? I DISCOVERED AN ANCIENT BOOK WRITTEN BY MY ANCESTOR, GERONIMO STILTONOOT! HE CARVED HIS STORIES INTO STONE TABLETS AND ILLUSTRATED THEM WITH HIS ETCHINGS.

I AM PROUD TO SHARE THESE STONE AGE STORIES WITH YOU. THE EXCITING ADVENTURES OF THE CAVEMICE WILL MAKE YOUR FUR STAND ON END, AND THE JOKES WILL TICKLE YOUR WHISKERS! HAPPY READING!

Geronimo Stilton

WARNING! DON'T IMITATE THE CAVEMICE. WE'RE NOT IN THE STONE AGE ANYMORE!

HURRY, GER!

The sun was shining on *Old Mouse City*. Down by the port, the rays were as HOT and **golden** as cheese sauce. Boats from all over the world were docked at the port, and the place was crawling with rodents *rushing* here and there.

That morning I had an important task to carry out: I was in search of slabs of rock! I, **GERONIMO STILTONOOT**, know a little something about rocks. Every week I stock up on slabs of **MARBLE** for *The Stone Gazette*, the newspaper that I run. (Yes, we call it a newspaper, even though paper hasn't been invented yet.)

Some mice say that *The Stone Gazette*'s news is really **Heavy**. And by "heavy," they mean that it weighs a lot! Each issue is **etched** into really heavy slabs of rock, like the one I am chiseling this into now. The slabs are **HARDER** than a hunk of stale cheddar!

As I walked through the port, my **CARTOSAURUS** followed me. He is the dinosaur that helps me transport heavy loads. We stopped in front of a tall pile of **STONE SLABS**. A mouse popped out from behind the pile, **SURPRISING** me.

"I assure you that this is the **best** stone you will find in all of Old Mouse City!" he exclaimed, picking up a slab of marble to show me. But I wasn't so sure. It didn't look much **THICKER** than my tail!

"To tell the **truth**, it looks a bit

4

CARTOSAURUS

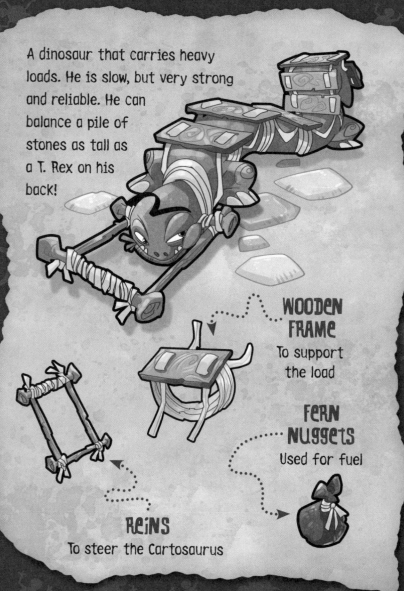

A dinosaur that carries heavy loads. He is slow, but very strong and reliable. He can balance a pile of stones as tall as a T. Rex on his back!

WOODEN FRAME
To support the load

FERN NUGGETS
Used for fuel

REINS
To steer the Cartosaurus

It's an excellent slab!

Well ...

FRAGILE," I told him. "Fragile? Nonsense! This slab could support a T. REX!" the merchant bragged.

As we tried to make a deal, I heard a loud ROAR. My sister, Thea, had trotted up on Grunty, her autosaurus. She can't ever seem to control that beast: When she SKIDDED to a stop, her dinosaur STOMPED on my poor cartosaurus!

"HURRY, GER, JUMP ON!" Thea yelled. "We have to get to Trap's tavern right away!"

Before I could OBJECT, Thea lifted me onto the saddle and RACED off at full speed toward the Rotten Tooth Tavern. It's run by our cousin Trap, and is the most popular tavern in Old Mouse City. (Maybe because it's the only one!) Fossilized feta, what was the hurry?

QUIET BACK THERE!

Breathless, I followed Thea inside the tavern. I couldn't believe my eyes. BONES AND STONES! I had never seen it so **CROWDED**, not even for the annual prehistoric joke championship!

An ENORMOUSE crowd of rodents filled the tavern. They quietly listened to a **tiny, tiny** voice coming from the other end of the room. Thea easily made her way up to the front, but I am not as good with crowds as she is. I couldn't see a thing, so I bravely tried to move forward.

"Um, excuse me," I asked, tapping the mouse ahead of me on the shoulder. "Can

8

you please tell me who is speaking?"

He didn't even bother to turn around.

"Excuse me!" I said loudly.

"Shh! Keep quiet back there!" someone called out.

I turned purple with embarrassment. It was all that RUDE mouse's fault!

I tried to get around the rude mouse, but he was too WIDE.

"Ahem!" I said.

Can you believe that rodent still ignored

me? **Furious**, I decided to push right past him.

BONK! I hit my head on an arm as hard as **GRANITE**. That's because it really *was* granite!

Instead of a mouse, I had **bumped** into a statue of Rattney Dangerfur. He is the most famouse **comedian** in all of prehistory.

And I had mistaken him for a real, fur-and-whiskers rodent.

WHOOPS!

Then my cousin Trap popped up behind me. He was sipping a stinky **bean**-and-**skunkweed** juice that he waved under my snout.

"Geronimillo!" he said. "Are you here to listen to my **celebrity** guest?"

"**YUCK!**" I cried. I pushed away the disgusting **slop**. "What celebrity?"

"What do you mean, 'what celebrity'?" Trap **snorted**. "Where do you live? In a **CAVE**?"

Geronimillo!

Hee, hee!

A STRANGE RODENT was listening to us. He had white fur with gray stripes. I had never seen him before.

"You should be ashamed of yourself!" he scolded, **waving** his club under my snout. "We don't need any **ignorant** mice in this place."

"Who are you, anyway?" I asked.

"**HEY!** Can you please be quiet back there?" It was the tiny voice from before.

Trap started dragging me right up to the celebrity guest. I was so embarrassed!

I was even more embarrassed when I recognized who it was: Paleo Pickax, the famouse **explorer**! That's why Thea had brought me there. I had been trying to interview him for months.

Trap thrust me forward. "Professor Pickax, this is the **chattermouse**!"

PALEO PICKAX

HE IS THE MOST FAMOUSE EXPLORER IN OLD MOUSE CITY. (PROBABLY BECAUSE HE IS THE ONLY ONE!) HE IS KNOWN THROUGHOUT THE PREHISTORIC WORLD FOR HIS AMAZING ADVENTURES.

MOST IMPORTANT DISCOVERIES:

- THE LOST CITY IN THE SECRET VALLEY OF THE MYSTERIOUS ISLAND

- THE COUNTRY HIDEAWAY OF THE CITY AUTOSAURUS

- THE CAVE OF DISCOUNT FOSSILS

- THE TORTOISE SHELL OF DOOM

Leave it to Trap to **RAT ME OUT**!

"Forgive him," Trap continued. "He is jumping out of his **fur** with excitement. He wants to know about your latest **exciting** discovery!"

Paleo Pickax looked me up and down. He was a very short mouse with a white **BEARD** and **MUSTACHE**.

"I understand, but there is no reason for him to **yell** like a shoutosaurus," he said coldly.

Trap chuckled. **ACK!** How could I have been so **RUDE**?

"This discovery is the most important one of my career," Pickax continued. "As you know, my latest expedition was to the **LAND OF ICE**."

The Land of Ice! **Brrr!** That region is completely covered with ice and snow. Just thinking about it makes my tail freeze!

"I was on a GLACIER when I noticed a strange movement on the horizon," Pickax went on. "I looked more closely, and what I saw was truly incredible!"

We were hanging on his every word.

"There, between the snowcapped mountains, was a . . . a . . ."

ZZZ-zzz-ZZZ-zzz-ZZZ

ZZZ-ZZZ-Z

Is he asleep?

I don't know!

Right before our astonished eyes, Pickax had fallen asleep! He was snoring like a hibernating POLAR BEAR!

I noticed that the strange rodent who had called me ignorant was sleeping, too. Everyone else started to whisper at once. WHAT had the famouse explorer seen between the snowcapped mountains of the Land of Ice?

AN AMAZING DISCOVERY

We waited and waited, but Pickax didn't give any sign of **waking up**. Slowly, the crowd began to clear out. Thea, Trap, and I stayed, and the STRANGE RODENT with the striped fur was still napping.

Among the mountains ...

Huh?

Suddenly, Pickax SNAPPED AWAKE! He began to speak again, as if nothing had happened.

"Among the **snowcapped**

mountains, there was . . . *a moving mountain!*" he announced loudly. "A giant **MOUNTAIN** covered in snow that **WALKED**, just as if it was alive!"

I couldn't believe my **furry** ears. As far as I know, since this world has existed, mountains **DO NOT WALK**! (I admit that the world has not existed for very long, but still!)

"I will return to the Land of Ice to find the **secret** of the walking mountain," he said. "This discovery will be a scientific **TREASURE**!"

Right at that moment, the striped rodent next to me woke up with a **START**.

"A treasure?" he cried. But before I

What?! A treasure?!

could tell him about the walking mountain, he **RAN** out of the tavern.

I didn't think much of the STRANGE RODENT'S bizarre behavior. I suddenly remembered that I needed to purchase those **MARBLE SLABS**, or the newspaper would not come out in time! I slipped away and met up with my CARTOSAURUS back at the port.

As I finished loading up the slabs, Thea walked up to me.

"Geronimooo!" she sang out.

I shuddered. When Thea uses that tone, either I have to go on some dangerous mission, or she needs a favor.

Either way, it's a bad sign!

"Professor Pickax gave me an interview!" she bragged. "He is definitely going back to the Land of Ice to uncover the mystery of the walking mountain. And guess what? HE LEAVES TOMORROW!"

Then she winked, which is a *really* bad sign.

I gulped, getting ready for the bAd news. "Well, this is all very interesting, but —"

"Oh, I *knew* you would be interested!" Thea interrupted me. "That's why Professor Pickax said that I could accompany him, and bring you with me!"

I turned as WHITE as mozzarella.

I have great news for you!

Um...

21

"But I can't leave," I objected. "I have, um, a bunch of things to do."

Thea looked at me **suspiciously**. "Like what?"

I thought quickly. I had to avoid getting *DRAGGED* into another **DANGEROUS** adventure. "Well, I have to **dust** the cave, and fix up the archives. . . ."

"Oh, that stuff is no fun, Geronimo!" Thea said. "You'll have a **MUCH BETTER** time with me in the Land of Ice! I've already told everyone that in the next edition of *The Stone Gazette* there will be a piece on the **WALKING MOUNTAIN**. I need you to take notes!"

"But, Thea, I — um — I threw out my back the other day," I lied. "The shaman has forbidden me to carry heavy **SLABS** of stone, so I can't take any notes."

Thea didn't look like she believed me. Then her gaze fell on the **pile of stones** I was loading onto my cartosaurus.

"Well, these stones are THIN and light," she said. "So you shouldn't have a problem."

I could imagine my whiskers turning into ICICLES when we got to the frosty Land of Ice.

"But I can't even chisel!" I protested. "I've got **calluses** on my paws. And I jammed my elbow when I was rock bowling!"

Suddenly, a cloud of SMOKE appeared and surrounded us like a fog.

Um . . . I jammed my elbow!

"**AAACK!**" I yelled, waving my arms above my head.

"FIRE! FIRE! FIRE! THE GREAT ZAP! WE'RE DOOMED!"

I ran away, but when I looked behind me, I realized there wasn't any fire. The gust of smoke was coming from a stick held by a rodent named **SCORCH**. His job is to look after Old Mouse City's **fire reserve**, and he was doing his regular rounds.

Scorch's job has two parts: He **lights** the fires all over the city and makes sure they don't go out. For that reason, he is important to the **SURVIVAL** of all of us cavemice. But poor Scorch never gets any sleep, and he's always very *nervous*!

SCORCH

HE LOOKS AFTER
OLD MOUSE CITY'S
FIRE RESERVE.
HE'S IN CHARGE OF
LIGHTING THE FIRES
IN THE VILLAGE AND
MAKING SURE THEY
DON'T GO OUT.

APPEARANCE:
BAGGY EYES

PERSONALITY: THE
WORST! HE IS VERY
RUDE BECAUSE HE IS
ALWAYS SO TIRED —
HE NEVER SLEEPS.

PASSION:
GORGONZOLA ICE-CREAM CAKE

The smoke **faded** quickly, and I saw Thea eyeing me curiously.

"You look pretty **spry** for a mouse with a bad back and a jammed elbow," she said.

Embarrassed, I **blushed**. "Well, I seem to be feeling a *little* bit better. . . ."

"**PERFECT!**" Thea cried. "We leave tomorrow!"

I moaned. "Thea, I am just not up for another **DANGEROUS** adventure!"

"Well, there's another reason why you absolutely must come," she

said. "Paleo Pickax is **BENJAMIN'S** idol, and he is coming with us!"

At that point I didn't have any more **excuses**. Thea knew that I would do anything to make my nephew Benjamin happy! She had trapped me.

Thea went home to pack her bags, and I made my way to the newspaper office. **Strangely**, I had the feeling that someone was watching us. . . .

Heh, heh, heh!

VOYAGE TO THE LAND OF ICE

The next day, we boarded a BOAT and headed up the Dino River. Benjamin was so excited to be going on the trip that he was practically JUMPING out of his fur. As soon as he hopped on board, he began to bombard Pickax with questions.

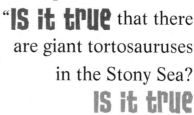

"IS it true that there are giant tortosauruses in the Stony Sea? IS it true that the waves at Boulder Beach can reach three hundred tails high? **IS it true** that there is a stinkosaurus that is so stinky that the smell knocks out anyone who comes close?"

The old explorer **patiently** answered Benjamin's questions.

"Yes, the shells of the tortosaurus are **BIGGER** than the head of the T. Rex! And the waves are really, really tall! And I myself have smelled the stink of . . ."

ZZZ-zzz-ZZZ-zzz-ZZZ

Pickax had fallen asleep in the middle of his sentence!

As for me, I wasn't chatting at all. I suffer from **seasickness**, and my tummy was doing somersaults.

Thea tried to distract me. "Come on, Ger, think of all the beautiful landscapes you will see."

That was exactly what I *didn't* want to think about. It's so **cold** in the Land of Ice that even the fleas have fur. BRRR! Also, this region is the home to the POLAR CLAN, the ferocious club-bearing white bears trained by Tiger Khan — chief of the mice-eating saber-toothed tigers. YIKES!

Just thinking about those scary bears made me tremble with fear. I was trembling so hard that I woke up Pickax.

"BY MY WHISKERS! THESE WAVES SURE ARE HUGE!"

I don't know which was worse: my nausea or my fear. So I fainted!

But the trip continued on, despite my TUMBLING TUMMY and my shakes. Finally, we reached our destination on the third day.

1 A little sick

2 Really sick

3 Really, really sick!

ICICLES ON MY WHISKERS

The **LAND OF ICE** is far away, wild, unexplored, endless, but most of all . . . **ICY! BRRR!** As soon as we hit land — that is, ice — my tail **froze**!

We piled on a double layer of **furs** and then followed Pickax across the ice. Even though he carried an **enormouse BAG** on his back,

the old explorer was as **fast** as a rat chased by a cat!

"Move it, you lazy

rodents!" he called back to us as we struggled to keep up with him. "It's a long hike to the snowcapped mountains. *Faster! Faster!*"

"Come on, Ger, get a move on!" added Thea, because I, of course, was far behind everyone else.

"But . . . **HUFF** . . . walking in the snow is very tiring . . . **PANT** . . . and I am not used to it . . . **PUFF!**" I panted.

"What a CHATTERMOUSE you are, Mr. Stiltonoot," Pickax said. "The cold, crisp air is perfect for brightening your outlook. Yours seems to be a bit gloomy, and I don't like that at all!"

I didn't answer him, mostly because I wanted to save my BREATH. I knew I would need it for the hike, and I was right!

In the next several hours, we had to (in order):

1 Climb a really **Steep** cliff. I slipped and almost went extinct!

2 Walk on a rock bridge as **THIN** as a slice of Swiss. Eek!

3 March against some strong, **freezing** winds . . . how tiring!

Pickax stayed in front of us the whole time, and he seemed to be having a lot of **FUN**! I, on the other paw, had **ICICLES** on my whiskers, throbbing and swollen paws covered in blisters, and a permanent **SQUINT** due to the **BRIGHT LIGHT** reflected from the snow. **GREAT**

ROCKY BOULDERS, I was falling to pieces!

Besides that, I kept having the strange sensation that I was being followed. But whenever I turned around, I didn't see anyone.

Finally, we all stopped to rest. Pickax examined the ice underneath us.

"Hmm, this place isn't suitable for our TENTS," he declared. "It isn't protected well from the cold, and it's on too much of a slope."

"Let's move on and find a better spot," suggested Thea.

"Nooooooooo!" I yelled. I could not take one more step. "This place will do *just fine*. The snow is very comfortable. Look!"

To prove it, I JUMPED onto a pile of frozen snow. It was harder than petrified cheddar! I'm pretty sure I bruised all of my **BONES**, but I didn't **COMPLAIN**, because I didn't want to have to start hiking again.

Pickax took off his pack and began to **rummage** through it. "Well, if you say so, Stiltonoot, we'll stay right —"

"YAAAAAAAHHHHH!"

A high-pitched yell echoed through the valley.

"By my whiskers! Can't you ever let me finish a sentence, chattermouse?" Pickax **scolded** me.

"It wasn't Uncle Geronimo," responded Benjamin. He pointed to a spot down in the valley. "It was . . . **them**!"

I looked into the valley and, filled with terror, I saw them — the **POLAR CLAN**,

Tiger Khan's allies in the Land of Ice. They were an army of the most WILD and FEROCIOUS polar bears!

A STEP AWAY FROM EXTINCTION!

The bears of the Polar Clan were not alone. At the head of the group, in fact, was someone who looked **familiar** to me. But where had I seen him?

Slowly, as the army got closer, I got a better look at him. He didn't look like a polar bear. He had WHITE FUR with gray stripes. . . .

"Hey!" Thea said with a start. "That mouse was at the Rotten Tooth Tavern!"

Of course! It was the strange STRIPED RODENT! Only he wasn't a rodent at all. He was a ferocious saber-toothed TIGER. One of Tiger Khan's soldiers, I'm sure.

PETRIFIED PROVOLONE!
THAT SNEAKY CAT HAD
TRICKED US!

The tiger had disguised himself as a mouse.
I *knew* someone had been following us!

SABER-TOOTHED TIGER

DISGUISE

FAKE RODENT

TIGER KHAN must have sent him to Old Mouse City as a **SPY**. He must have been on our tails this whole time, with a herd of **HUNGRY BEARS** behind him.

I began to tremble so hard the snow under my feet started to move.

"Stay still, you scaredy-mouse!" Pickax yelled. "If you keep shaking like that, you'll cause an **AVALANCHE**!"

Benjamin came to my rescue. He hugged me really tightly and I stopped shaking. Oh, how I love my nephew! Meanwhile, the Polar Clan got closer and closer.

"YAAAAAAAHHHHH!"

"Grab those dirty rats!"

"We'll turn them into meatballs!"

"No — mouse omelets!"

"No — rodent stew!"

The bears began to fight and hit one another with their clubs.

"**QUIT IT!**" the tiger yelled. "You aren't supposed to hit each other. You're supposed to hit **THEM**!" He pointed at us.

Meanwhile, Pickax was pulling stuff out of his bag: a **SLINGSHOT**, whisker shine ointment, a coconut helmet, six **CHEESE FOSSILS** ...

"Hmm," he muttered to himself, "that's not it. . . . **Where did I put them?**"

"What are you **LOOKING** for, Professor?" asked Thea impatiently. "**Hurry**, the bears

43

are getting closer and closer!"

She wasn't kidding — I could see the yellow glow of their **ferocious** eyes! Even though they were big and bulky, they easily moved through the deep snow.

CHEESE FOSSIL

SLINGSHOT

WHISKER SHINE OINTMENT

Where did I put them?

"They're going to pick us up and **CHOMP** on us like cheese puffs!" I yelled. "We need to . . ."

I was too afraid to finish my sentence.

For the love of cheese! **WE WERE A STEP AWAY FROM EXTINCTION!**

Polar Clan, attack!

Roar!

SKI CHAMPIONS!

"Here they are. Finally!" Professor Pickax exclaimed. He held up some very long STRIPS OF WOOD, and tall poles made of bone. "We will escape the bears with these!"

He handed two poles and two strips to each of us. We stared at him, perplexed. How could these help us escape a group of HUNGRY, fanged bears?

Pickax put a piece of wood under each of his feet and strapped them on with strips of **leather**.

"Do as I do!" he urged. "These skis were given to me many years ago by the Ipsqueaks, a **peaceful** and kind rodent tribe that lives around these parts."

Thea and Ben put on their skis, and I thought they looked so FUNNY! Then, when I put mine on, I thought they looked like TOOTHPICKS on my paws. I was still confused about how they would help us escape the Polar Clan.

But how do they hook together?

Pickax approached Thea. "Let me explain how they work. You bend your knees, and then launch yourself **DOWN** the slope. Be careful not to lose your balance. With these on our feet, we will move faster than a **TURBO VELOCIRAPTOR**! We will lose those polar bears in a flash."

Thea looked excited. She launched herself forward and began to quickly slide down

Woohoo! I'm going so fast!

the **slope**, moving left and right to avoid hitting any bumps in the snow.

Benjamin didn't think twice, either. He *PUSHED OFF* and followed his aunt, ZIPPING around the snow expertly.

Professor Pickax hoisted his bag on his shoulders and got ready to SPEED down the slope. I, on the other hand, was having second thoughts. It looked pretty **dangerous**!

Pickax folded his arms *impatiently*. "Hurry up, Stiltonoot, or you'll become CLAN GRUB!"

"Um, is there any other way to lose those bears?" I asked nervously.

I looked down at the skis. "These **SKINNY** pieces of wood don't look like they could support a **flea**, much less me!"

"**BUCK UP**, Stiltonoot!" Pickax said, giving me a pat on the back. An instant later . . .

WUUAAAAAAAAAAAAAAAH!

. . . I went **hurtling** down the slope with him!

We got away from the Polar Clan with only seconds to spare! Even though they looked like furry dots behind us, we could still hear them.

"SLIMY SNOWBALLS!
HOW ARE THEY SO FAST?"

"THOSE AREN'T MICE, THEY'RE VELOCIRAPTORS!"

"ROAR! WE LET THEM GET AWAY!"

Toooo faaaast!

Then I heard the tiger exclaim with an angry roar, "What will happen to the treasure? **TIGER KHAN WILL BE FURIOUS!**"

Wait a minute, I thought. **TREASURE?** *What treasure?*

Fossilized feta! That's why Tiger Khan's spy had followed us all the way here. The tigers thought that Pickax had found treasure! Because he was napping, that **cheesebrain** had only heard the last words of the explorer's speech: *"This discovery will be a scientific treasure!"* He totally misunderstood Pickax!

Luckily, the **SHOUTS** of the bears faded in the distance. We were safe . . . or were we?

Pickax had forgotten to teach us how to **ST◉P**!

Squeak! There were big rocks waiting for

us at the bottom of the cliff. If I crashed into them, I'd be extinct!

Out of control, I zipped past Thea and Benjamin.

"HEEEEELP! STOOOOP MEEEEE!"

I missed a TREE by a hair. Then I skied over a ROCK, and like a giant ramp, it sent me shooting in the air.

Heeeeelp!

SPLAT! I landed in a pile of snow, making me look like a yeti. But I kept going . . . and was heading right for the cliff's edge!

I tripped on my skis and ROLLED AND ROLLED down the hill, quickly becoming a giant snowball. Holey cheese! I was about to roll off the cliff!

Suddenly, I didn't feel anything under my

paws anymore. Was I still alive?

BOOOOOOOOOOONK!

I smacked into something. When I opened my eyes, I saw that I had hit an enormouse block of ICE. I had been spread out against it like **cream cheese**! I pulled myself off and shook my head, **dazed** and **confused**. What had happened to the cliff?

Squeak!

BOOOONK!

Wh-where a-am I?

I was sore and FREEZING, but at least I had saved my fur! Then I looked behind me and saw that I had skied over the CLIFF after all! It wasn't as HiGH as I thought it was.

In fact, Thea, Benjamin, and Pickax each

soared over it with a carefree jump, landing next to me without a WHiSKeR out of place.

"Uncle Ger, you were awesome!" Benjamin said, hugging me.

"Yes, well, um — it was easy," I declared, trying to hide the fact that I was shaking.

Thea looked up at the sky. "It's getting **dark**," she pointed out. "We should set up camp."

Pickax pulled two **TENTS** out of his bag. He was about to tell us how to set them up when he suddenly stopped, staring at a point behind us. His face turned as PALE as mozzarella.

"Th-th-there it is!"

GOOD-BYE, PREHISTORIC WORLD!

Pickax pointed to the horizon, petrified.

I followed his gaze and my eyes opened wide.

"The mo — mo —" I stammered, too shocked to get the words out.

"The mosquito? What does that have to do with anything?" asked Thea as she brushed snow off her jacket.

"There can't be any mosquitoes in this cold," observed Benjamin wisely.

"N-n-no," I said. The sight in front of my eyes had fried my brain like a mozzarella stick! I struggled to get the words out. "The mou — the mountain is moving!"

Thea and Benjamin turned around, and then they saw it, too.

In the setting sky, between the peaks of the massive mountains, a snowy white **MOUNTAIN** *moved* with a slow and steady pace. Just like it was walking! We stared at it, FROZEN, and then we looked at one another in shock.

The mountain is moving!

Finally, Pickax broke the spell and exclaimed, "We found it! We found it!"

Then he grabbed Thea and Benjamin by the paw and jumped up and down triumphantly. Caught up in the moment, I stepped on my tail. So I began to jump up and down

next to them . . . because of the **pain**!

"It will be the greatest **scoop of the millennium**!" added Thea happily, thinking of the story she could write.

Just then, the sun began to set and a *frigid* breeze sprang up. But Pickax didn't seem to notice.

"Let's follow that mountain!" he cried.

"Yaaawn!" Benjamin was tuckered out. "I am prehistorically tired!"

"YAAAWN!" echoed Thea.

So tired!

"Yaaawn!" I added. "The mountain seems far away. Can't we follow it in the morning?"

Pickax frowned. "Well, I suppose it is better if we leave tomorrow when we are rested and *fresh*. Now let's set up camp."

We set up the tents: one for Thea, and one for me, Benjamin, and Pickax.

"Sooner or later, I have to learn how to build one of those IGLOOS that I have seen the Ipsqueaks make," sighed a tired Pickax.

He *curled* up in a fur sack near the entrance of the tent, while Benjamin and I **snuggled** up in the back.

"I can't wait until **dawn** so we can go after the mountain," Pickax mumbled with a yawn.

"You can say that again!" Benjamin said. He was tired and **excited** at the same time. "Will it be hard to follow it?"

But Pickax had already fallen asleep. His response was loud and musical:

zzz-zzz-zzz-zzz-zzz...

Benjamin and I covered our ears, but it was no use.

"This is going to be a **ROUGH NIGHT**, Uncle!" Benjamin said as Pickax's powerful **SNORE** shook the tent. And if that wasn't enough, the freezing wind **howled** through the mountains like an angry cat.

WHAT A NIGHTMARISH NIGHT!

Benjamin and I huddled together to keep warm.

"Good night, Uncle!" he whispered to me. "I am so excited that we found the mountain!"

"Me, too, my little mouseling! Good night!" I replied, tucking his **sleeping bag** under his chin.

Exhausted by the events of the day, we finally fell asleep — but not for long. The tent began to shake, tossed around by the wind!

Benjamin awoke with a start. "Uncle, can you feel it, too? The tent is moving!"

"Calm down, dear nephew, everything will be fine," I said. But I wasn't so sure.

Then we heard Thea's voice through the **HOWLING** wind. "**GET OUT OF THERE!** The wind has **picked up** my tent!" she continued. "It's about to do the same to yours!"

We bolted out of our sleeping bags and headed for the exit. But Pickax, who was still snoring loudly, was **BLOCKING** it!

RIIIIP! The wind pulled the stakes right out of the snow, and the tent lifted off the ground. We were fluttering through the air!

"**GERONIMOOOO! BENJAMIIIIIN!**" Thea yelled desperately as she watched us **SOAR** through the sky.

I *TUGGED* on Pickax's whiskers, trying to wake him.

"**PROFESSOR!** You can't sleep at a time like this!" I yelled.

"Five more minutes . . ." the explorer **mumbled**.

I gathered my courage

Get out of there!

and poked my snout
through the opening
of the tent.

PETRIFIED
PROVOLONE!

Frozen with terror,
I watched as the tent
took us **DOWN**
to the valley. Then the
wind swirled us in
the direction of the
mysterious moving
mountain!

Benjamin and I exchanged fearful glances.

"PROFESSOR! PROFESSOR! WAKE UP!"

I tried everything I could to wake him up. I **pinched** his cheeks. I shook his shoulders. I **YELLED** loudly into his ears.

"Yes, yes, go on ahead. I will catch up," he muttered in his sleep. Then he rolled over, making the tent SWAY even more dangerously.

Meanwhile, the sky began to light up with the colors of dawn. I looked out of the tent and saw the MYSTERIOUS MOUNTAIN approaching rapidly. In a few seconds, we would hit it and get squashed as flat as sliced cheese! We'd make a perfect FROZEN MEAL for the Polar Clan.

I closed my **eyes** and grabbed on to Benjamin, preparing for the **crash**.

"Good-bye, prehistoric world!" I cried.

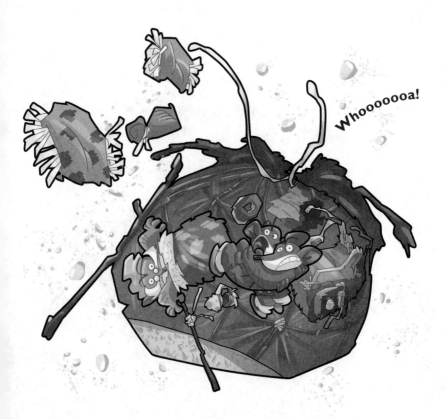

Whoooooooa!

BONK AND BADABAM!

To my surprise, we didn't crash. We did **tHUD** into something — it was solid, but it was actually . . . **soft**!

We bounced off the soft thing and landed on the ground. The **fluffy** snow broke our **FALL**, and we stood up with barely a whisker **OUT OF PLACE**.

Benjamin and I stepped over Professor Pickax, who was still sleeping, and climbed out of the tent. A pure white landscape **stretched** out before us.

My head was **SPINNING** so much that I felt like my tail was where my nose should be and my ears were where my paws should be!

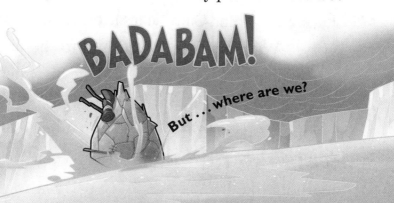

BADABAM!

But . . . where are we?

Then Pickax climbed out of the tent, **yawning** and stretching. "My word, Stiltonoot, what a *restless* sleep you had! You kept moving and hitting me like a T. Rex with **HICCUPS**!"

Benjamin giggled as I tried to explain. "Actually, it was the wind. . . ."

"Tell me about it later," the explorer said. "I need to **STRETCH** my legs a bit!"

He quickly *DARTED* off. Benjamin and I exchanged worried glances. What if there were Polar Clan bears around here, or worse? We quickly followed him to the big, soft wall that our **TENT** had hit when we crashed.

"Hmm," he said thoughtfully. "What kind of a MOUNTAIN is this? I've never seen anything like it."

He reached out with his paw and touched

the wall. "It seems to be covered with this mossy white stuff," he observed. "It's almost like . . ."

"Like fur?" Benjamin asked.

Suddenly, a TERRIBLE noise shook the ground under our feet.

ROOAAAAR!

It almost seems like . . .

ROOOAAAR!

The sound became more and more deafening.

ROOOAAAR!

Ben pointed upward, his eyes wide. We followed his gaze and saw that the **FURRY** mountain had a head! The cry was coming from an **enormouse mammoth**!

Thick white fur covered its body. It had two long, curved **TUSKS** that ended in **SHARP** points. And it sounded very angry!

"**AHA!**" exclaimed Pickax triumphantly.

ROOOAAAR!

"We didn't see a mountain moving. We saw a **great woolly mammoth** moving! And this one has rare white fur! What a discovery!"

ROOOAAAR!

The mammoth roared again. It was so **LOUD**, it made our whiskers tremble.

"Um, **nice** little woolly mammoth," I said, slowly backing away from the beast. "We'll go away and leave you alone, okay? Just stay calm."

Paleo, is that you?

To our surprise, the **snout** of a cheerful rodent popped out from under the mammoth's white fur.

"**PALEO?**" he asked. "Paleo Pickax, is that you?"

"Yes, it's me," Pickax answered cautiously. He **squinted** to get a closer look at the rodent.

The cheerful rodent **grinned** and jumped out of the mammoth's fur. We stared at him curiously. He wore a light-colored **fur** suit with a hood that covered his head.

He had the most **dazzling** smile I had ever seen. We could see that he was a very friendly mouse.

"It's me! Chipper Cheeryfur!" he exclaimed, opening his arms to welcome us.

THWACK!
THWACK!

At first, it didn't LOOK like Pickax recognized the name. But Chipper kept smiling, and finally the explorer's face **brightened**.

"Chipper Cheeryfur! It's really you! It's been so long!"
Pickax threw himself on Chipper, giving him a **rough** hug.

Chipper responded

THWACK!
THWACK!

Good to see you!

by **THWACKING** Pickax on the back.

"My friend, how WONDERFUL to see you again!" Chipper exclaimed. "What are you doing here?"

"I came back here to uncover the **mystery** of the moving mountain, dear Chip," Pickax explained. "Are you here by yourself?"

In answer, Chipper **whistled** loudly, and immediately, tons of **snouts** poked out from the mammoth's fur.

"Welcome, strange mice!" the rodents exclaimed in unison.

Then they jumped off the mammoth to **greet** us. It was a big, **confusing** mess of hugs and pats on the back.

By the time they were done, my shoulders were as **red** as lava from the Cheddar Volcano!

"We are **Ipsqueaks**.

It's a pleasure," said Chipper.

"It's been years since we've seen each other, Chipper," said Pickax. "What's been happening?"

Chipper Cheeryfur **sighed**. "Ah, it's been difficult! The POLAR CLAN ran us out of our valley. They wouldn't let us live in **peace**. Then, one day, we saved a baby **woolly mammoth** from drowning in a frozen lake."

It's been difficult!

He pointed to the enormouse mammoth behind him. "Here she is! Our beloved **CASHMERE**. She is a rare example of a **WHITE** mammoth. Most other mammoths have dark fur."

"*That* mammoth is the one you found?"

And lift!

Oof!

asked Benjamin in disbelief. Chipper nodded. "She had ventured out onto the surface of the lake, but her weight broke the ice and she fell into the water! It took every single one of us to hoist her onto dry land. From that day on, Cashmere became our friend. She helps us get around."

He looked up at Cashmere. "She looks tough, but she is very **sweet**!"

"Was she that big when you found her?" I asked.

"Oh, no!" said Chipper. "She was as **small** as a hill then, and she grew to be as **tall** as a mountain. It's helpful, because we can hide ourselves in her fur every time DANGER is near."

CASHMERE
2 months old

CASHMERE
2 years old

CASHMERE
20 years old

"The Ipsqueaks are **happy** and **peace-loving** rodents," Pickax explained to me and Benjamin. "They prefer to avoid conflicts, especially with the Polar Clan."

"Cashmere always defends us when those hungry bears are around," added Chipper. "You should see how they scramble when they see her! Ha, ha, ha!"

All the Ipsqueaks began to **laugh**. It was contagious, and Benjamin and I started to laugh, too. Those happy little mice had put us all in a **good mood**.

Pickax walked up to Cashmere to examine her more closely. "Fascinating!" he said. "I have never seen a mammoth this size!"

He shook his head. "To think I mistook her for a WALKING MOUNTAIN!"

Then he pointed at me. "Excuse me, I haven't introduced my friend GERONIMO

Stiltonoot and his nephew **Benjamin**. They have accompanied me to take notes on this expedition and spread the **NEWS** of this extraordinary discovery to all of Old Mouse City!"

A murmur of **disapproval** spread among the Ipsqueaks.

Chipper shook his head. "**No, no, no! please!** We can't let Cashmere get famouse! Then **everyone** would want to come meet her, and our peaceful lives would be ruined by curious onlookers!"

You cannot reveal our secret!

No, no, no!

BONES AND STONES, WE HADN'T THOUGHT OF THAT!

Chipper was right. We couldn't reveal the secret of Cashmere and betray such a **peaceful** group of rodents.

We were about to reassure them when we heard a familiar voice **YELL** from the distance.

"Ooh, finally! I found you! Here you are!" Benjamin lit up. "Aunt Thea!"

My sister was running toward us across an icy ridge. She was **flailing** her arms and she seemed very alarmed.

"Hurry!" she urged. "We need to get out of here. I was following your tent as it flew through the air, and bears from the

POLAR CLAN spotted me. They are still on my tail!"

Terrified, we looked toward the horizon. The Polar Clan was **marching** toward us!

We've got to run!

THE REVENGE OF THE POLAR CLAN!

The **Ipsqueaks** quickly climbed onto Cashmere's back and **HID** under her fur. Only then did Thea notice the enormouse mammoth.

"**Holey cheese!** Is that the walking mountain?" she asked.

Cashmere made a loud, **TRUMPETING** noise, nodding her furry head.

"That's not all," I told Thea. "She may also **SAVE** our fur. Come on!"

I pulled her aboard the trunk of our giant new friend. Cashmere LIFTED us onto her back. Then she did the same for Benjamin and Pickax.

Then we hid, fearfully waiting for the Polar Clan to arrive.

Seconds later, they crossed the icy ridge. Then they stopped, petrified at the sight of Cashmere.

Some of the bears took a step back.

"Where did that rodent hide herself?" one asked.

"It's like she disappeared into thin air!" said another.

Come on!

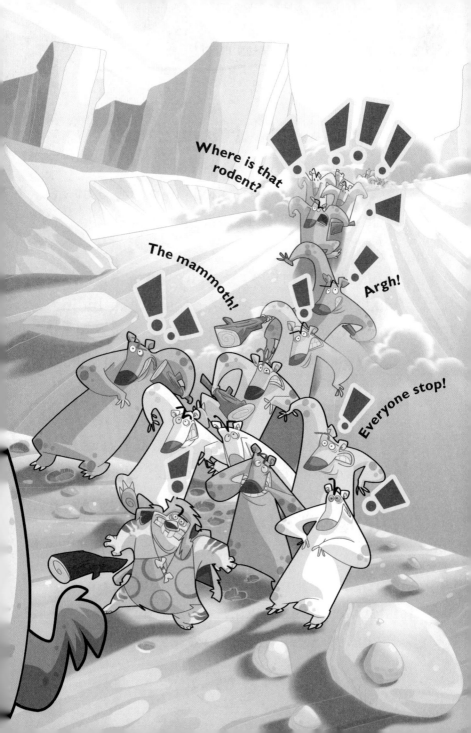

"So where's the **treasure**?" asked one bear.

"I don't know," replied another. "But at least we found that stinky mammoth."

"ATTACK!"

As the bears surged forward, Chipper made a sign and all the Ipsqueaks hiding under Cashmere's fur sprang into action as **quickly** as velociraptors. They grabbed on to the mammoth's long **tufts of fur** and pulled themselves up to her belly.

"Stay strong!" Chipper yelled up to us.

A frozen silence fell over the Clan. Then one of them shouted, **"OH NO! SHE'S GOING TO DO IT AGAIN!"**

"Take cover!" a bear yelled.

Thea and I were confused, but an instant later we understood. . . .

The Ipsqueaks began to scratch Cashmere's

94

belly, **tickling** her. The mammoth started to snicker, first quietly, but the sound grew louder and louder. She exploded in a **powerful** trumpeting sound that echoed all around us. Then she jumped up and down, making the earth tremble beneath her.

ROOOAAAR!

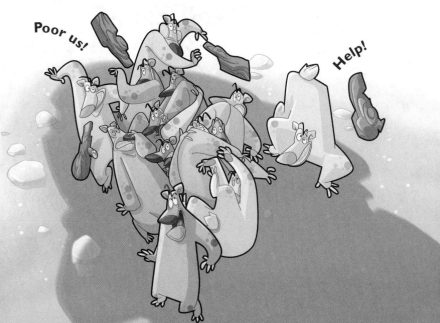

Poor us!

Help!

Even the mountains began to vibrate.

"We need to get out of here!" cried one of the bears.

But it was too late. An enormouse mass of snow CASCADED down from the shaking mountains like a rushing wave of water. The avalanche SLAMMED into the bears,

I want my mommy!

pushing them out of the valley. We heard the bears cry out as they were **swept away**.

"Save yourselves!"

"HEEEELP!"

"Good-bye, Polar Clan!"

Then they disappeared into the distance.
We were saved!

HMM, HMM, HMM . . .

Very relieved, we climbed down from the mammoth's back. I was as green as moldy cheese: With all that bouncing, I had ended up getting mammoth sick!

Thea introduced herself to our new friends, and petted Cashmere to thank her. The mammoth **blushed**.

"ENOUGH CELEBRATING!" Pickax burst out. "We need to decide what to

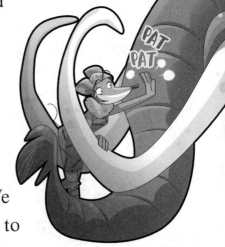

Good job, Cashmere!

PAT PAT

tell the rodents of Old Mouse City about the WALKING MOUNTAIN."

"I don't think we should say anything," I proposed. "If we reveal Cashmere's **secret**, we will put the lives of all the Ipsqueaks in danger. They just want to live in peace!"

Pickax frowned. "But I **promised** everyone I would reveal the secret," he said. "They will be **disappointed**."

"There has to be a solution," Thea chimed in. "I'm sure Geronimo will think of another **article** to publish about the expedition that's just as exciting."

"But — I —" I stammered.

Grateful, Cashmere planted a powerful **kiss** on my cheek with her trunk.

"That **tickles**!" I cried, jumping up.

Chipper Cheeryfur ran up to me and started shaking my paw vigorously. "Thank you so much, Mr. Stiltonoot!" he said. "You will be our SAVIOR!"

My mind was **racing** faster than a cavemouse toward cheese. I wasn't sure what to say.

GREAT ROCKY BOULDERS! THIS WAS A REAL DILEMMA!

I suppose I could say that we never found the walking mountain. But I don't like to lie. On the other paw, if I told the truth, it would hurt the Ipsqueaks!

I had a prehistoric problem on my paws!

I sat on a snow-covered rock and tried to think of a solution.

HMM, HMM, HMM . . .

Meanwhile, Thea, Benjamin, and Pickax cuddled up in Cashmere's fur to take a **nap** before heading back to Old Mouse City. Then Pickax started **snoring** so loud that I couldn't think!

ZZZ-zzz-ZZZ-zzz-ZZZ

I couldn't take it anymore, so I climbed up onto Cashmere's back.

ZZZ-zzz-ZZZ-zzz-ZZZ

It was no use! Pickax's snore carried through the icy air.

That's when I got an EXTRAORDINARY IDEA!

I quickly woke up Thea and Benjamin. (I didn't bother trying to wake up Pickax — I knew that even pulling his *tail* wouldn't work.)

"We need to get to Old Mouse City right away!" I said, excited. "More precisely, we need to contact Gossip Radio!"

"Gossip Radio? But that radio station is RIDICULOUS," Thea pointed out.

"Exactly," I said. "I think I know a way to tell *everyone* what happened **without Lying** — and that will still keep the Ipsqueaks safe."

"What do you have in mind, Uncle?" Benjamin asked.

I winked at him. "You'll see!"

We said good-bye to Chipper Cheeryfur, the Ipsqueaks, and Cashmere, promising that we would never REVEAL their secret.

Cashmere managed to wake up Pickax with a big tickly **kiss**. Then we put on our SKIS and slid into the valley, headed toward Old Mouse City.

A STROKE OF GENIUS!

When we reached *Old Mouse City*, I led Thea and Benjamin to Gossip Radio, the radio station run by **SALLY ROCKMOUSEN**. This station works in a really bizarre way!

You see, Sally brags about spreading **truthful** news to all the citizens of Old Mouse City. But her radio station actually always **distorts** the truth!

Hee, hee, hee!

It works like this: Sally's spies (she calls them reporters) hear some **gossip**. Usually, they are eavesdropping! One spy *squeals* to another spy, who *squeals* it to another spy, and so on.

What happens is that each mouse who hears the news **changes** it in some way. By the time it gets to Sally, the news has **transformed** into something totally different! Basically, telling something to Gossip Radio is the best way to keep it a **secret**.

With Gossip Radio, I could tell the story of the WALKING MOUNTAIN without lying, and then write an article about something else. So I hid under Radio Rock and yelled:

"THE WALKING MOUNTAIN IS A GIANT FURRY BEAST!"

Sally's reporters quickly picked up the scoop. Then they started to pass it along. . . .

"THE WALKING MOUNTAIN IS A GIANT PILE OF LEAVES!"

" . . . IT'S A GIANT RIND OF CHEESE!"

" . . . IT'S A GIANT CHUNK OF MELTING CHEDDAR!"

Thea and Benjamin were holding their stomachs from laughing so much.

It was a genius idea!

"**Nice job, Ger!**" Thea complimented me. "That was a great idea."

"Yes, Uncle, it was a stroke of genius," agreed Benjamin, hugging me.

Within minutes, everybody in Old Mouse City was talking about a mountain made of **cheese** that **melted** all over the Land of Ice.

Pickax was disappointed that he had to keep his **discovery** a secret. But he vowed to keep his promise to the Ipsqueaks and **PROTECT** them and Cashmere from the Polar Clan.

Since I had told the truth about the walking mountain (even though Gossip

Radio had **twisted** it), I was free to write a different article about the **LAND OF ICE** for *The Stone Gazette*.

I wrote about the peaceful, kind, and very useful **woolly mammoth** species. I even etched a **PORTRAIT** of Cashmere, although only you and the Ipsqueaks would recognize her. The article was a huge popular **success**!

It's a rat-tastic article!

Since then, when we have the time, Benjamin, Thea, and I go to **VISIT** Cashmere and the Ipsqueak tribe. Cashmere always greets us by **squeezing** us with her trunk and covering us with kisses. The Ipsqueaks welcome us with powerful **THWACKS** on the back. But we don't mind, because they are our good friends.

I promise to tell you about those other stories soon, or I'm not . . .

Geronimo Stiltonoot, cavemouse!

Don't miss any adventures of the cavemice!

#1 The Stone of Fire

#2 Watch Your Tail!

#3 Help, I'm in Hot Lava!

#4 The Fast and the Frozen

Up Next!

#5 The Great Mouse Race

MEET
GERONIMO STILTONIX

He is a spacemouse — the Geronimo Stilton of a parallel universe! He is captain of the spaceship *MouseStar 1*. While flying through the cosmos, he visits distant planets and meets crazy aliens. His adventures are out of this world!

#1 Alien Escape

#2 You're Mine, Captain!

Don't miss any of my other fabumouse adventures!

#1 Lost Treasure of the Emerald Eye

#2 The Curse of the Cheese Pyramid

#3 Cat and Mouse in a Haunted House

#4 I'm Too Fond of My Fur!

#5 Four Mice Deep in the Jungle

#6 Paws Off, Cheddarface!

#7 Red Pizzas for a Blue Count

#8 Attack of the Bandit Cats

#9 A Fabumouse Vacation for Geronimo

#10 All Because of a Cup of Coffee

#11 It's Halloween, You 'Fraidy Mouse!

#12 Merry Christmas, Geronimo!

#13 The Phantom of the Subway

#14 The Temple of the Ruby of Fire

#15 The Mona Mousa Code

#16 A Cheese-Colored Camper

#17 Watch Your Whiskers, Stilton!

#18 Shipwreck on the Pirate Islands

#19 My Name Is Stilton, Geronimo Stilton

#20 Surf's Up, Geronimo!

#21 The Wild, Wild West

#22 The Secret of Cacklefur Castle

A Christmas Tale

#23 Valentine's Day Disaster

#24 Field Trip to Niagara Falls

#25 The Search for Sunken Treasure

#26 The Mummy with No Name

#27 The Christmas Toy Factory

#28 Wedding Crasher

#29 Down and Out Down Under

#30 The Mouse Island Marathon

#31 The Mysterious Cheese Thief

Christmas Catastrophe

#32 Valley of the Giant Skeletons

#33 Geronimo and the Gold Medal Mystery

#34 Geronimo Stilton, Secret Agent

#35 A Very Merry Christmas

#36 Geronimo's Valentine

#37 The Race Across America

#38 A Fabumouse School Adventure

#39 Singing Sensation

#40 The Karate Mouse

#41 Mighty Mount Kilimanjaro

#42 The Peculiar Pumpkin Thief

#43 I'm Not a Supermouse!

#44 The Giant Diamond Robbery

#45 Save the White Whale!

#46 The Haunted Castle

#47 Run for the Hills, Geronimo!

#48 The Mystery in Venice

#49 The Way of the Samurai

#50 This Hotel Is Haunted

#51 The Enormouse Pearl Heist

#52 Mouse in Space!

#53 Rumble in the Jungle

#54 Get into Gear, Stilton!

#55 The Golden Statue Plot

#56 Flight of the Red Bandit

The Hunt for the Golden Book

Be sure to read all my adventures in the Kingdom of Fantasy!

THE KINGDOM OF FANTASY

THE QUEST FOR PARADISE:
THE RETURN TO THE KINGDOM OF FANTASY

THE AMAZING VOYAGE:
THE THIRD ADVENTURE IN THE KINGDOM OF FANTASY

THE DRAGON PROPHECY:
THE FOURTH ADVENTURE IN THE KINGDOM OF FANTASY

THE VOLCANO OF FIRE:
THE FIFTH ADVENTURE IN THE KINGDOM OF FANTASY

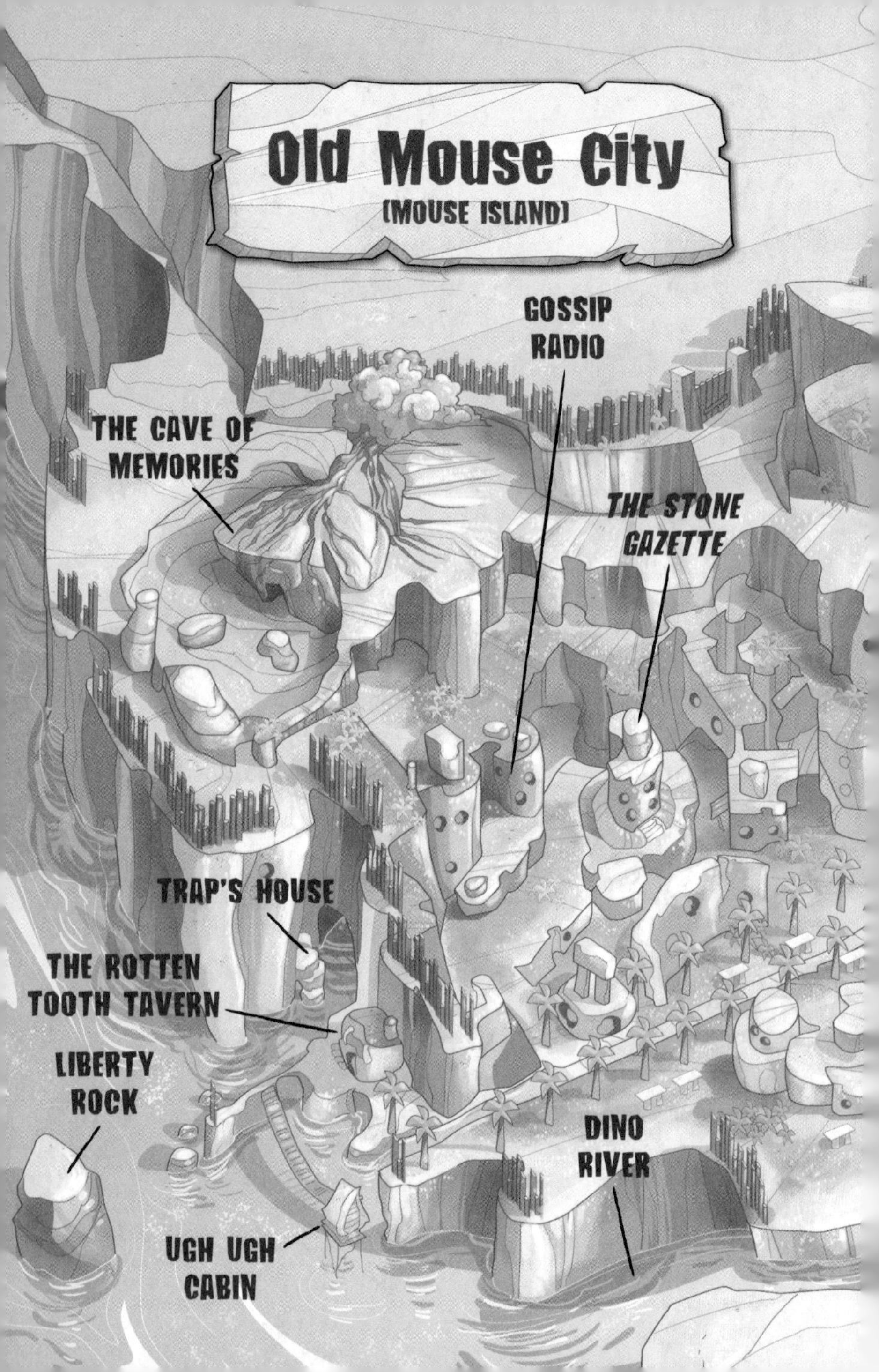

Old Mouse City
(MOUSE ISLAND)

GOSSIP RADIO

THE CAVE OF MEMORIES

THE STONE GAZETTE

TRAP'S HOUSE

THE ROTTEN TOOTH TAVERN

LIBERTY ROCK

UGH UGH CABIN

DINO RIVER

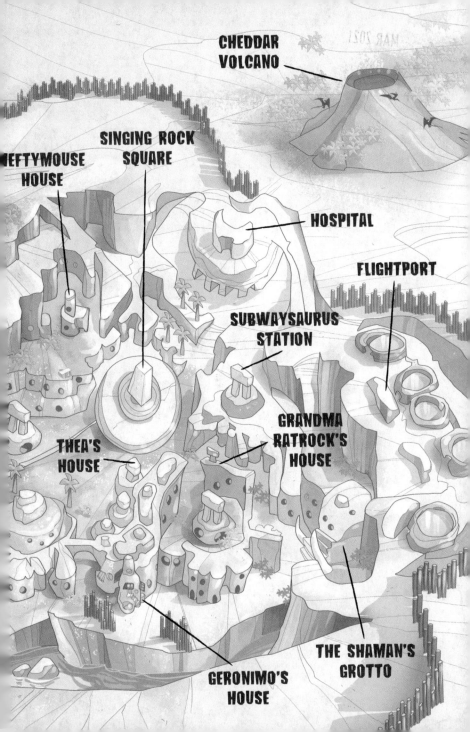

CHEDDAR VOLCANO

SINGING ROCK SQUARE

LEFTYMOUSE HOUSE

HOSPITAL

FLIGHTPORT

SUBWAYSAURUS STATION

GRANDMA RATROCK'S HOUSE

THEA'S HOUSE

THE SHAMAN'S GROTTO

GERONIMO'S HOUSE

MAR 2021

DEAR MOUSE FRIENDS,
THANKS FOR READING,
AND GOOD-BYE UNTIL
THE NEXT BOOK!